The Three Princes and the Magic Carpet

Sweet Cherry

THE ARABIAN NIGHTS

CHILDREN'S COLLECTION

First published in the UK by Sweet Cherry Publishing Limited, 2023
Unit 36, Vulcan House, Vulcan Road,
Leicester, LE5 3EF, United Kingdom

Sweet Cherry Europe (Europe address)
Nauschgasse 4/3/2 POB 1017
Vienna, WI 1220, Austria

2 4 6 8 10 9 7 5 3

ISBN: 978-1-78226-838-3

The Arabian Nights Children's Collection:
The Three Princes and the Magic Carpet

Text based on translations of the original folk tale,
adapted by Kellie Jones
Illustrations by Grace Westwood

www.sweetcherrypublishing.com

Printed and bound in India

Long ago, in the ancient lands of Arabia, there lived a brave woman called Scheherazade. When the country's sultan went mad, Scheherazade used her cleverness and creativity to save many lives – including her own. She did this over a thousand and one nights, by telling the sultan stories of adventure, danger and enchantment.

These are just some of them …

The Sultan
The ruler of India

Prince Hussain
The sultan's eldest son

Prince Ali
*The sultan's second
eldest son*

Prince Ahmed
*The sultan's
youngest son*

Princess Nourinnihar
The sultan's adopted daughter

Pari Banou
A genie

Nisha
A sorceress

Schaibar
Pari Banou's brother

Chapter 1

The Story of the Three Princes and the Princess

There once was a sultan of India who had three sons. From oldest to youngest, they were called Prince Hussain, Prince Ali and Prince Ahmed. Alongside Princess Nourinnihar, they were the sultan's pride and joy.

Princess Nourinnihar was not the sultan's daughter. She was the

---

sultan
A type of ruler or king in Islamic countries.

daughter of his oldest friends. But they died when the princess was only twelve, so the sultan took her in and raised her with his sons of a similar age. Hussain grew up to be competitive. Ali grew up to be clever. Ahmed grew up to be creative. Nourinnihar, whom they nicknamed 'Nour', grew up to be beautiful, charming and kind. It was no wonder that by the time she was old enough to marry, all three brothers were in love with her.

'But you cannot all marry her,' their father pointed out one day,

when the young people were
playing board games.

'Who says I want to marry
any of them anyway?' the princess
said tartly.

'Come on, Nour,' Hussain chuckled. 'I know I am your favourite.'

'But you always have to win everything.' She looked pointedly at the game she had just lost.

'What about me?' said Ali. 'You always beat me.'

'At games maybe, but not arguments. You are a complete know-it-all.'

Meanwhile, Ahmed was too busy staring dreamily at Nour to say anything at all. In his imagination, they were already married.

'Do you want to marry someone else?' the sultan asked. 'To marry into a different family?'

'No!' Nour said quickly. 'I love it here.' And in truth she loved all the princes, too, each in their own way.

'There is no hurry, is there?' she asked. 'I thought the princes wanted to go travelling.'

'That is true,' said Ali. 'Maybe we can kill two birds with one stone.'

'I propose a competition!' Hussain cried.

The princess rolled her eyes. 'Of course you do.'

'Or a treasure hunt,' Ahmed

said. 'Imagine all the wonders that must be out there ...'

'Very well,' said Nour. 'You will all go travelling as planned. On your way you will look for the rarest objects you can find and bring them back to me at the end of a year. Then I will decide which gift and which prince I like best.'

'A year of peace and quiet?' said the sultan. 'What an excellent idea!'

The princes left the city the next day disguised as merchants. They spent the first day's journey

merchant
Someone who buys and sells goods.

together and slept the night at an inn. The next morning the road they were on divided into three.

'See you back here in a year, then,' said Ali.

'Not if I see you first!' said Hussain.

'I just hope a year is enough!' said Ahmed. 'I want to see as much of the world as I can.'

Then the princes mounted
their horses, and each took a
different path.

Chapter 2

The Story of Prince Hussain

Prince Hussain, the eldest brother, headed southeast towards the coast. He had heard many stories of the strength and riches of the kingdom of Bisnagar, and so he crossed deserts, mountains and farmlands to reach it. After three months of hard travel with various caravans of real merchants, he arrived in

caravan
A band of people and animals travelling together, often formed for safety when crossing a remote area like a desert.

a bustling city. It had a gate at each end, a palace in the middle and streets lined with shops everywhere between.

Each street specialised in selling a different thing and was shaded from the sun with vaulted ceilings of stone or covers of draped cloth. One street sold only fabrics, including the finest linens from India, dyed all the colours of the rainbow or painted with scenes of people, places and flowers so vivid that they looked real. On the same street were silks and

brocade
A fabric with a raised, woven pattern.

brocades from Persia, China and beyond. The next street over sold porcelain from China and Japan that was so fine Hussain could almost see through it. Another sold carpets of all different sizes, many so beautiful that he would hate to walk on them.

A street full of goldsmiths and jewellers dazzled him with lustrous pearls, diamonds, rubies, emeralds and other precious stones. Despite the stories he had heard, Hussain was still amazed to see so much treasure in one place. It was not

Persia
An ancient empire in southwestern Asia, now called Iran.

only the city that seemed to be rich, but its people. Other than the holy men and women who had given up such worldly goods, there was not a single person who did not wear or carry something beautiful. Many had ornaments around their necks, wrists or ankles, garlands of flowers on their heads or sweet-smelling nosegays in their hands. The scent of flowers filled the air, both because of the wandering rose-sellers and the bouquets placed in vases at almost every shop.

nosegay
A small bunch of sweet-smelling flowers.

'Surely,' Hussain said to himself, 'I will find something here that will win Nour's heart.'

But he did not buy anything the first day, or the second, returning each time to the inn where he was staying, which was popular with travelling merchants.

'Empty-handed again?' one merchant remarked on the third day, when they were in the inn's central courtyard. 'Does nothing take your interest?'

'*All* of it does!' said Hussain. 'I have never seen clothes, jewels, flowers or furnishings finer than the ones I have seen here. But to be honest with you, I am looking for something I have never seen *at all*. Something new. Something rare.'

Something worthy of a princess, he added silently.

The search continued for a month, until one day Hussain saw a man with a dirty carpet folded over one arm.

'Thirty gold pieces!' the man called out. 'Thirty for this carpet!'

Blinking at the high price, Hussain looked again. The carpet was only four square metres, and that square was almost worn through in places. He was not surprised that no one stopped to take the man up on the offer.

'Why,' Hussain asked him, 'would anyone pay twice the amount for this carpet when there are the most beautiful carpets in the world nearby?'

'Because they should be paying ten times the amount for mine,' said the man.

Hussain smirked. 'And why is that?'

'Because those carpets may be beautiful, but this carpet is magic.'

'A magic carpet?' said Hussain,

the doubt clear in his voice. 'Does it speak, perhaps?' Then the prince bent his head towards the carpet and whispered, 'Hello, I do not mean to be rude, but you need a wash.' He laughed at his own joke.

'No, it does not speak,' said the seller, unsmiling. 'But it understands certain things all the same.'

'What things?'

'Come with me and I will show you.'

Hussain followed the man through the streets, out of the covered shopping quarters and into an open space where there were no people and the carpet could be laid out on the ground. It looked even worse under the sun, dull and thin, with the pale fringes that tied off the yarn at the ends tangled together in places.

'Perhaps I misunderstood you,' said Hussain. 'Were you in fact offering to *pay* thirty gold pieces for someone to take this thing off your hands?'

'The price just went up to forty,' said the man, unsmiling *and* unimpressed.

'It must be a remarkable carpet indeed,' said the prince, trying to be less rude. It was very possible that the man was ill, in which case he should be kind until he went on his way.

'This carpet,' said the man, 'will fly you anywhere you want to go.'

'Amazing,' said Hussain, not believing a word. 'Flying must be a most convenient way to travel. No rivers to cross, mountains to climb – can you fly through clouds or must you go around them?'

'There are no obstacles in the sky. Any journey can be done in a fraction of the time it would take by camel or horse.'

'I see.' Hussain was trying not to laugh, but it was difficult. 'How does it work exactly?'

'You simply sit on it and say where you want to go.'

'Like this?' said Hussain, about to walk onto the carpet. But the man stopped him.

'Forty pieces of gold,' he repeated.

'But you cannot expect me to buy it without proof!'

The man nodded – 'Very well' – and stepped onto the carpet first.

'Carpet, rise.'

The carpet rose into the air, and Hussain's jaw almost dropped to the floor. The man held out his hand and Hussain stepped onto the carpet with him.

'Carpet,' the man said again, 'take us to wherever this young man is staying.'

The carpet lurched forwards
and Hussain abruptly fell on
his bottom. They flew fast, the
carpet rippling over the air and
the wind playing with its fringe.

The next instant, they were there
in the courtyard of Hussain's inn.
Hussain immediately ran into his
room and took a purse full of gold,
far more than forty pieces.

'You are right,' he gasped on
his return. 'This carpet is worth
ten times as much as any other –
more. Please accept this, and my
apologies for not believing you.'

The man took the heavy
purse and left, smiling. Hussain,
ever competitive, immediately
commanded the carpet to take
him back to the crossroads where
he and his brothers had parted

four months ago. This time the journey seemed to take minutes, not months. He stayed at the nearby inn and made the people who worked there record the date and time of his arrival, so that his brothers would know by how long he had beaten them back.

But I need not wait here for them, he thought to himself. *My quest may be over, but my adventure need not be.*

The next morning Hussain mounted the carpet again and named a place so far away that he never imagined he could go there and come back within eight months. But now he had a magic carpet, and it took him not just there and back, but to many other distant lands. Each time he returned to the inn to find his brothers not yet there, he would set off again.

'Truly,' he declared, when he returned from his final destination, almost exactly a year since he left home, 'with this carpet there can be no question of who will win Nour's heart!'

And he settled down to wait for his brothers, confident in the extreme that neither of them could possibly have found a gift greater than his …

Chapter 3

The Story of Prince Ali

Prince Ali, the middle brother, headed west into Persia with the first caravan he came across. He had read much about the capital city Shiraz, which was a melting pot of different people, cultures and – he hoped – *treasures*. The merchants he travelled with knew of his quest, though not that he was a prince. They assured him that

Shiraz was home to the rarest and finest items from around the world, which was why they were going there too.

'Perfect,' Ali replied, 'that is exactly what I am looking for.'

Something as rare and fine as Nour herself, he added silently.

After four months of travel, during which his legs felt permanently moulded to his horse's back, Ali arrived in Shiraz. The first thing he did was write to the princess, who shared his fascination

assured
To assure someone of something is to give them confidence and remove their doubts around that topic.

with the place. Next he visited the famous bazaar. It was a huge building, buzzing with voices and arched over with pillars. Along the walls, inside and out, were countless shops, with sellers who shouted loudly that they had the best brocades, gold, jewels, silks and spices on offer. But unlike his older brother, Ali was not impressed.

To one seller he said, 'Do you truly sell the finest silverwork in all the world?'

'Yes, I do,' the man said proudly.

bazaar
A Middle Eastern marketplace made up of shops and stalls.

'See for yourself.' And he waved at the shop behind him. It shone like an armoured knight from the West, the polished silver mirroring anyone who passed.

'Is the man in the shop next to yours a liar?' asked Ali.

The seller looked startled. 'Excuse me?'

'Well, he said that *he* sold the finest silverwork in the world. In fact, five other men said the exact same thing. Are they all liars too?'

'No,' said the seller.

'Then are *you* a liar?'

'No!'

'But how can six different men each sell the best silverwork in the world?'

'Well … I …'

When the seller could find no answer, Ali moved on. The bazaar was a place to get lost in, and he did.

Daily he searched. Weekly he wrote to Nour. And eventually over a month had passed, in which it seemed to Ali that he had inspected and rejected every object on sale in Shiraz. He knew all the shopkeepers by name and the merchants who traded with them. And they all knew to show him any new treasures they found before they showed them to anyone else. But at the end of six weeks, Ali still had not found anything truly unique, and the only shops he had not visited were the ones that sold ivory.

ivory
A hard, off-white material that forms the tusks and teeth of elephants and other animals.

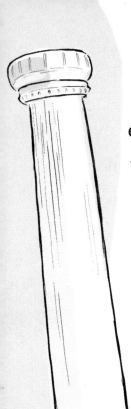

Nour loved animals,
especially elephants. She
would not want a piece of
one as a present, but one
day Ali was pulled into
a shop that sold nothing
else. There were beautiful
carved cups and knife
handles, beaded necklaces
and smoking pipes, bottles
and boxes. However,
the item the ivory seller
thrust at Ali was a
plain tube about thirty
centimetres long and
three centimetres wide.

42

'Yours for thirty gold pieces!'
he said.

'Are you mad?' said Ali. 'I could
buy anything in this shop for less.'

'Nothing that is magic.'

'Magic?' Ali scoffed. 'There is no
such thing! I believe only in what
my eyes can see.'

'Perfect,' said the seller, handing
him the tube. 'Then look through
this. It will show you whatever you
want it to.'

Ali turned the tube in his
hands, discovering that each end
was plugged with glass. 'Then I
suggest *you* use it to find a stupider

customer than I am,' he said, handing it back.

'The price just went up to forty.'

Sighing, Ali held the tube to his eye. He did not think of Nour deliberately. She was just always on his mind. He was constantly wondering how she was doing and if she was missing him. The moment he looked through the glass, he gasped.

He could see the princess laughing
with her maids in the palace back
home, looking healthy and happy.
How he had missed her smile!
Next, Ali thought of the sultan.
And there he was! The prince
grinned to see his father frowning
at his advisors.

'This is amazing!' Ali cried. 'I will take it!'

He handed the seller a heavy purse, which held far more than forty gold pieces. The shopkeeper was delighted, and so was Ali. This was an even better gift than he had hoped to find. He could not wait to see Nour's face when he gave it to her.

He journeyed back to the crossroads where he had parted with his brothers, and thereafter to the inn where he found Hussain waiting. His older brother looked smug, but Ali did not care. As he settled down to wait for Ahmed to join them, Ali had no doubt that his gift would beat both his and Hussain's ...

Chapter 4

The Story of Prince Ahmed

Prince Ahmed headed north, searching parts of Persia that are now known as Pakistan and Afghanistan for a gift for Princess Nourinnihar. Unlike Prince Ali, when he could not find anything that interested him, Ahmed moved on quickly. This was because he wanted to see as much of the world as he could within the year.

His third stop was Uzbekistan and the city of Samarkand, which was on the Silk Road, an ancient trade route linking China with the West. Samarkand was well known for its holy places, but Ahmed admired its arts and crafts, including silks and ceramics, carpets and embroidery, calligraphy and painting. He bought several of these for himself but found nothing for Nour.

Eventually Ahmed decided that he would have to return home empty-handed or arrive late. *Perhaps,* he thought, *I will find*

calligraphy
An artistic style of handwriting, often very beautiful.

something on the way back, and it will be even more special for appearing at the last minute.

He went to buy food for his journey and passed a poor man sitting on the ground. He had a wooden bowl in front of him to collect food and money, but it was empty. He was very thin, with a nasty cough that seemed to wrack his whole body.

Ahmed decided to give the man some food once he had some. He had bought some rice and was just considering some fruit when a woman offered him an apple.

'Thirty gold pieces!' she said.

Except for her sparkling green eyes, the woman's face was covered. Ahmed could not tell if she was joking, but he burst out laughing anyway. 'Friend, I am not *that* hungry!'

'Oh, but this apple cannot be eaten anyway.'

'Then your price is even more ridiculous!'

'Ridiculous for an ordinary apple,' the seller agreed. 'But this apple is magic.'

'Magic?' said Ahmed, the word catching his attention. He looked at the apple more closely. It was red and glossy, but it did not appear to be anything special. It was not even very big. 'What does it do?' he wondered.

'It can cure any illness. One sniff of this apple will restore a person to perfect health.'

Ahmed took and sniffed the apple. He could smell nothing but a subtle fresh green smell, and since he was in perfect health already, there was nothing for the reported magic to heal.

'If what you say is true,' said Ahmed, 'then this apple is magic indeed, and thirty gold pieces would be too cheap.'

'You are right,' said the seller, quickly, 'I meant to say forty.'

'My brothers like to tease me and say that I am easily fooled. Are you trying to fool me?'

'No, sir! This apple was made by one of Samarkand's greatest healers. She used her knowledge of plants and medicine to grow an apple tree, which produced only two apples. One will never leave this city. This one she is willing to sell.'

Ahmed was very tempted, but he remembered the time that Hussain and Ali had tricked him into believing that the palace was haunted. He had later complained to Nour who told him that there were no such things as ghosts. What would she say about a magic apple?

'I will not believe what you say without proof,' Ahmed declared.

The fruit seller called over several local men and women who were shopping at the market. Each confirmed that one or the other of the two magic apples had cured them or their loved ones in the past.

'This is not what I meant,' said Ahmed. 'I want to see the apple cure someone with my own eyes.'

'Who?' asked the seller.

'Him.'

Ahmed pointed to the poor man he had passed. He was coughing again, but the moment Ahmed took the apple to him and told him to smell it, the coughing stopped. The man's breathing became smooth and easy, with no painful rasping sound. The sickly yellow cast of his skin disappeared, as did the sheen of cold sweat. He still looked thin, but otherwise he glowed with good health.

'I feel better than I have in years!' he cried.

'You will feel even better after this,' said Ahmed, offering him the rice he had bought.

In the end, Ahmed paid far more than forty gold pieces for the magic apple, and he was happy to do so. Afterwards, he knew he should hurry home, but he could not resist a visit to the Ferghana Valley. It was reckoned to be a paradise on earth, and

once he had seen it, Ahmed had
to agree. He could have spent
days visiting its palaces and
daydreaming by its river.

I will have to bring Nour here one day, he thought. *As my wife, of course.*

Then Ahmed returned to the crossroads where he had said goodbye to his brothers, and then to the inn where they were waiting for him. He did not know what they had found that made them look so confident, but even his imagination could not think of anything better than a magic apple that cured the sick …

Chapter 5

The Story of the Three Princes and the Princess Continued

Since each brother was so certain of victory, they could afford to be kind to each other. They spent an evening at the inn in happy

companionship, talking about their travels and managing not to argue. Prince Ahmed went first, despite being the last back, Prince Ali went second and Prince Hussain went third.

When Ahmed learnt that Hussain had been the first one back and by how long, he said, 'Then you cannot have seen much of the world.'

'On the contrary,' said Hussain, 'I saw more of it than either of you did.'

'How is that possible?' asked Ali. 'Unless your visits were only very short.'

'Short? I was in Bisnagar for almost one month. Then I came

back here and went away again, visiting several countries where I stayed no less than two weeks.'

'That is impossible,' said Ali. 'Just going to Bisnagar and back would have taken you six months. You say you stayed there for one month, that makes seven months total. Did you *fly* to these other countries, brother?'

'Indeed, I did,' said Hussain.

'How?' asked Ahmed, who had once had an imaginary friend, now had a magic apple and was more likely than ever to believe that a man might fly.

'I will not tell you until you show me what gifts you have each found for Nour. It cannot be anything very big or I would have seen it.'

'Why should we show you ours if you will not show us yours?' said Ali. 'I hope for your sake that your gift is not that ratty old thing.' The "old thing" Ali was referring to was the carpet, the largest and easiest to see of the gifts.

'Indeed, it is,' said Hussain.

Ali laughed. 'I already knew you could not possibly beat my gift, but I thought at least you would *try*!'

The eldest prince just smiled. 'That carpet,' he said, 'may not look like much, but it can fly you anywhere you wish to go. It is a *magic* carpet.'

Ali and Ahmed looked at each other. If what their brother was saying was true, then he had a rare gift indeed.

'I have a magic apple,' said Ahmed. 'It heals whoever … smells it.'

'I have a magic … *tube*,' said Ali. His brothers both looked at him quizzically. 'It shows you anything you want to see.'

'Show me,' said Hussain. 'I want to see Nour.'

Ali and Ahmed watched as Hussain put his eye to one end of the ivory tube and looked through it. Ali expected him to be impressed. Ahmed expected him to be disappointed. Neither expected him to be horrified.

'No!' Hussain gasped, lurching to his feet.

'What is it?' asked Ahmed, snatching the tube.

'Give it here,' said Ali.

The tube showed Princess Nourinnihar, pale and still in her bed, the life almost gone from her eyes.

'She is dying!' gasped Ali.

Ahmed held up the magic apple. 'Not if we can get to her in time.'

Without saying anything, Hussain seized the magic carpet and ran with it outside the inn. He spread it across the floor. 'Get on!' he cried.

As soon as Ali and Ahmed were on board, the carpet zoomed forwards, whipping tears from their eyes with its speed – or maybe they were crying for a different reason.

Even at this rate, they feared they might not reach the palace in time. Ali, in particular, could not imagine a life without the princess. She did not have to be his wife.

She simply had to *live*. He prayed the whole way there that she would, even though what he had seen told him it was hopeless.

Hussain instructed the carpet to take them directly to Nour's balcony, then Ahmed raced to her bedside. He tried to make the princess smell the apple, but her eyes were closed. He held it by her nose, but she was breathing shallowly through her mouth, on the edge of death.

'Put some on her tongue,' suggested Ali.

Ahmed cut a tiny sliver of

apple and did so. On reflex, the
princess chewed. She swallowed.
As the princes watched, the colour
returned to Nour's cheeks, her
hair regained its shine and, finally,
her bright eyes opened.

'Welcome home,' she said.

The sultan was delighted at Princess Nourinnihar's rescue, and he could not have been prouder that his sons were the cause. But once the danger to her life was over, the princes turned their attention back to who might marry her when she was well enough. All except Ali, who spent most of his time talking and reading to Nour at her bedside as she recovered.

'Father,' said Hussain, 'who's gift do you think she liked best?'

'It was my apple that saved her life,' Ahmed pointed out.

'Only because my carpet got us here in time,' said Hussain.

'But you would not have known to come here at all without Ali's eye glass,' their father reminded them. 'I think it is a draw.'

'A draw?' Hussain frowned. 'That is the same as saying we all lost.'

'Or that you all won,' said the sultan.

'Same thing. We need another competition. One that will have a clear winner.'

'What about a shooting competition?' suggested Ahmed, who secretly thought that he was the best with a bow and arrow.

'Perfect,' said Hussain, who secretly thought the same thing. That was why he added: 'But rather than seeing who can get their arrow closest to the target, let us see who can shoot the furthest.'

'Very well,' said the sultan, before Ahmed could protest that Hussain was bigger and stronger than he was.

They went outside. While their father watched to make sure no

one cheated, a servant brought the princes' bows. Their quivers held twelve arrows, but they would only fire one each. Hussain went first, pulling the string back so far that it looked like the bow would snap. It cut the air with a *fwa* sound as it was released. The arrow sped to the far side of the palace gardens and lodged in the ground.

Next was Ahmed's turn. He pulled the string back as far as he could, until all the blood was driven from his fingertips and his arms trembled. Then he let go.

quiver
A case for carrying arrows.

The arrow followed the same path as Hussain's, but no one could see where it landed.

'I think it went further than yours,' said Ahmed.

Hussain looked annoyed,

for he thought the same thing. 'We need to get Ali,' he muttered.

But when they went to fetch Ali to take his turn, they found him and Princess Nour holding hands in her room. Ali was sitting on the edge of the bed, smiling into her eyes as she smiled into his. They did not even notice the arrival of the others.

'It seems there is no need to finish the competition,' whispered the sultan. 'Nour's heart has been won by other means.'

As soon as Nour was fully recovered, she and Ali were married. When the three princes had left on their adventures, Nour had been sure that she loved them all equally. But it had been Ali whom she missed most as time passed. Reading his letters had only heightened the feeling, and he had certainly sent more than either Hussain or Ahmed.

He knew her interests; he even shared many of them. He listened to her opinions, even if he sometimes argued against them. He cared about *her*, and not just winning her hand in marriage.

Truly he had given her the rarest gift, and it was not the ivory eye glass.

It was a happy ever after.

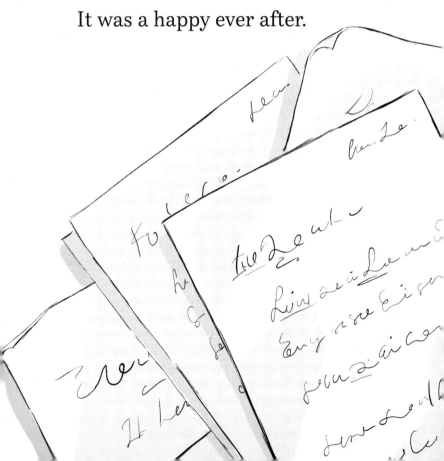

Chapter 6

The Story of Prince Ahmed and Pari Banou

The wedding of Prince Ali and
Princess Nourinnihar was a grand
and happy occasion for most
who attended it. But for Prince
Hussain it was a reminder that
he had lost. Luckily, as the eldest
son, his father was able to keep
him busy by training him to take
over as sultan one day. Now that
he had a flying carpet, there were

discussions about Hussain
travelling to build relationships
with other royal families.

'Perhaps,' his father suggested,
'you will even meet another
princess.' And so Hussain took off
for faraway lands.

For Prince Ahmed there
was no such distraction.
He stayed at home
moping, which involved
writing sad poetry and
asking the palace musicians to
play the saddest music every day.
When his father insisted that he
go outside to get some fresh air,

Ahmed took his bow and arrow and sank one after another into the target's dead-centre.

'I should have won,' he said to himself. 'Nour should have chosen me!'

This was not true, of course, for love is never won but given, and Nour had given hers to Ali. But still, Ahmed continued shooting until he ran out of arrows. Then he frowned at the empty quiver, realising that there had only been eleven arrows because he had used one for the shooting competition. It must still be out there somewhere, at the edge of the palace gardens. Huffing, Ahmed threw down his bow and went to fetch it.

The first arrow he found had black feather fletchings. It was Hussain's arrow. Ahmed smirked because he still could not see his own. He had indeed shot further than his eldest brother. To see how much further, he carried on walking. He wanted to get as far away as he could from the newlyweds, anyway. But eventually he was so far from the palace that he knew he must have walked right past his arrow.

No one can shoot this far, he thought. Then he saw an arrow buried in the side of some steep, craggy rocks. It was lit by a shaft of sunlight as if to say 'Look! Here I am!' And it had black-and-white feather fletchings so he knew that it was *his* arrow.

'That is impossible,' Ahmed said. He went to pull the arrow out of the moss. As he reached it, a sensation like walking through a spiderweb made his body tingle. The steep, craggy rocks became pure white boulders that glittered in the sunlight. The scene was both natural and manmade, with the boulders stacked like the craggy rocks had been, only taller and more orderly.

In the middle of the largest boulder was a doorway. And in the doorway, was a woman.

Ahmed took a step backwards in surprise. Again, he felt a tingling sensation. Then all he saw were craggy green rocks again. He stepped forwards, and there was the white palace of boulders. There was some kind of magical barrier separating the two.

'Are you a sorceress?' he called out to the lady.

'I am a friend,' she called back, holding out a hand to him.

---

sorceress
A woman who claims or is believed to have magic powers.

As Ahmed approached, he saw that the woman was very beautiful. She wore a long white dress that sparkled like the boulders. Diamonds ran along the parting in her dark hair and lay in a flower shape against her forehead. She smiled at him with bright green eyes and seemed so happy to see him that he forgot his nervousness.

'Ahmed,' she said warmly.

'Do you know me?'

'Of course! Do you not know me?' She covered the bottom half of her face with her shawl and magicked an apple out of thin air. *'Thirty gold pieces!'* she cried.

Ahmed gaped. 'You are the seller who sold me the apple in Samarkand?'

'I am more than that,' she said, dropping her shawl. 'Have you forgotten the little girl you played with as a boy?'

'I remember the *imaginary friend* I played with when my brothers ignored me,' Ahmed replied. 'Are you saying that you are her?'

'I am.'

'Then what was her name?'

'*My* name is Pari Banou.'

Ahmed gasped. 'It *is* you! My brothers said I was making you up!'

'Yes, well,' Pari sniffed, 'your brothers lack imagination. I do not like them much for making you doubt me.'

'Is that why you sold me the apple? You wanted me to beat them so that I could marry Nour?'

Pari shrugged. 'I just wanted you to beat them. I do not like

Nour much either. Between your brothers' teasing and her arrival, you stopped playing with me.'

'Forgive me.' Ahmed looked down guiltily. He realised that he still had the arrow in his hands and a thought struck him. 'It was you who made my arrow fly so far! Why did you do that if not to help me marry Nour?'

'To bring you to me,' Pari said simply. 'Now that I have, will you come inside?'

As Ahmed followed her inside the white boulder palace, he remembered the little girl he had played with years ago, before Nour started living with them. Whenever his brothers had said that they were too old for games, and just as Ahmed was wishing for someone else to play with, Pari would appear.

'You told me once that your father was a genie,' he remembered. 'Does that make you a genie too?'

'Yes, but my father is much more powerful.'

As they walked, Ahmed took in the surroundings. The inside of the boulder palace was mostly white like the outside, with occasional pops of green. Despite this, there was something cosy about the space. Green rugs gave the floors an almost mossy appearance, and all the furniture was made of pale wood.

They sat on a velvet couch with silk cushions and talked of many things. Time seemed to fly as they fell back into the easy rhythm of old friends. But they were just beginning to find a new rhythm – one that made Pari blush and brought back all of Ahmed's nervousness – when they realised that darkness had fallen.

'May I stay the night?' Ahmed asked.

Pari smiled. 'You may stay forever if you like.'

And Ahmed, who had no desire to return home or to leave such a lovely companion, thought "forever" sounded perfect.

Chapter 7

The Story of Prince Ahmed and Pari Banou Continued

The days that Prince Ahmed and Pari Banou spent together passed almost as quickly as the hours had done. Before long, they were married, and a great party was held that included all of Pari's family – except her brother who hated weddings.

Pari's father was huge and terrifying to look at, but he

welcomed Ahmed kindly into the family of genies. The celebrations lasted for a whole week with all manner of magical entertainment. There was food finer than any Ahmed had ever tasted, singers who played instruments he did not recognise and dancing that was almost dangerous in its enthusiasm.

At the end of it, Ahmed decided to visit his family, whom he had not seen since he followed his arrow away from the palace. They had not been invited to the wedding.

'I still have not forgiven your brothers for turning you against me as a child,' Pari had said. 'And what would they say about you marrying me? Not an imaginary friend but a *genie*? Even if they believe you, I am sure they will laugh.'

'They would believe me if you came too,' Ahmed suggested.

'The world is a dangerous place for genies. All anyone wants from us is what we can give them. I am safer here. In fact, do not even mention me. Just go to reassure them that you are alive and well after all this time.'

Reluctantly, Ahmed agreed.

Since he had no horse of his own, Pari magicked him one that was pure white all over. Then she magicked new clothes for him to wear and ten horsemen to go with him.

Ahmed promised to return soon. He took a path to the palace that led through the city first, letting the people see that he was home. They were so excited that they followed him, and Ahmed was so pleased that he handed out gold coins from the bottomless purse Pari had given him.

Ahmed felt bad for leaving home as suddenly as he had done, but the sultan was so relieved to see him that he forgave him at once. When Prince Ali and Princess Nourinnihar arrived, Ahmed was able to hug them both without being angry or jealous. He loved Pari differently to how he had loved Nour, whom he now saw as only a sister. Meanwhile, Prince Hussain was away travelling on his magic carpet.

'You look well!' said the sultan.

'I am happier than ever before,' Ahmed admitted.

'You must tell us everything!' said Nour. 'Where have you been?'

'And what have you been doing?' Ali added.

'I cannot tell you everything,' said Ahmed, 'but I promise I will one day. I just wanted to see you all.'

His father frowned. 'You mean you are not staying?'

'Only for a couple of days, but I will visit again, I promise.'

After months apart, even a couple of days with his youngest son was enough to make the sultan happy. Afterwards, Ahmed visited every month. Each time he went, Pari sent him in better clothes, on a finer horse, with even more horsemen. And he always gave money to the people as he passed them.

For his family he had other gifts. Some of them were things he had made himself: a painting in a gold frame for his father, a chess set hand carved from exotic woods for Ali and a book of magical stories Pari had told him that he'd written down for Nour. Other gifts included ornaments and jewels as fine as anything in the sultan's treasury.

This was all Pari's attempt to reassure Ahmed's family that he was living a good life. But it made the sultan's viziers whisper: 'What

treasury
A place where money and other valuable things are kept.

vizier
A high-ranking advisor to the royal family in the old Turkish empire and in Islamic countries.

is Ahmed hiding?' 'Where does he get such riches from?' 'Is he trying to buy your peoples' love? What next? *Your throne?*'

The sultan refused to be jealous of his own son. 'Ahmed loves me,' he told them. 'He would never do anything to hurt me – or his brother, Hussain, who will be sultan after me.' But he was increasingly curious about where the prince went when he left them. He sent for the sorceress Nisha to find out.

While the sultan believed that Nisha

worked for him, she actually had plans of her own. Much like him, she was also searching for someone who did not want to be found. Now she wondered if the two mysteries might be connected.

Since her magic was not strong enough to see through the barrier that hid Pari Banou's palace from the human world. Nisha waited until Ahmed visited his family again, and then followed him when he left. When they reached the craggy rocks where Ahmed had found his arrow, Nisha hid behind a tree. From there she watched the prince disappear and doubted her own eyes. Then she watched Ahmed's horsemen, now forty in number, vanish after him two by two. But when Nisha walked up to the same spot, the same thing did not happen to her. All she saw were the steep rocks covered in green moss, with no way up or through.

'There is something hidden there,' she later told the sultan. 'It will only reveal itself to people who are allowed to see it. If Your Majesty will give me more time, I will find a way in and bring you more information.'

'Very well,' the sultan agreed.

The next time Ahmed emerged
from the white boulder palace
with his horsemen, he found a
woman lying on the rocks. Her
clothes were torn and her skin was
muddy as if she had fallen there.

'Oh, thank goodness!' she cried

when she saw him. 'I thought nobody would ever come! Please, help me! I have been here for days.'

Ahmed helped the woman to stand, but when he tried to put her on a horse, she suddenly fainted. One of his men was forced to carry her inside the palace while Ahmed called for Pari.

'Back so soo–' Pari stopped speaking when she saw the woman, who was really the sultan's sorceress, Nisha. Her eyes had opened just in time to look curiously around her new surroundings.

So this is what was hidden behind the magic barrier, Nisha thought, taking in the glittering white courtyard.

'Forgive me, Pari,' explained Ahmed, 'but I found this poor woman just outside. May I leave her with you? My father is expecting me and I fear she is too weak to make the journey.'

'Water,' Nisha croaked. 'Please …'

Pari smiled, although it was not the sweet one Ahmed was used to. In fact, he thought it looked a bit angry.

'Of course, Ahmed,' she said. 'I know just the thing to help her.'

Then she said to the maids, 'Make our guest comfortable.'

Ahmed departed once more, and Nisha was moved to a beautiful room. It had a bed with a quilt of embroidered silk, sheets of the finest linen and covers of gold cloth. Pari herself propped the sorceress up with cushions of gold brocade and held a china cup to her lips.

'This is water from the Fountain of Lions,' she said as Nisha drank. 'It can cure any illness or injury ...'

'I feel better already,' said Nisha, since she had no real illness or

injuries to speak of, except for a
blister on her foot.

'… but it takes half an hour
to work,' Pari finished.

'Of course,' said Nisha, trying to cover her mistake. 'I only meant that my thirst is gone. My aches and pains remain.'

'Then I will leave you alone to rest,' said Pari.

That gave Nisha thirty minutes to explore what she could of the palace, which was not much since the maids kept telling her to lie back down. When the time was up, even her blister had healed. She said her thank yous to Pari and left, eager to tell the sultan of her discovery.

Chapter 8

The Story of Prince Ahmed and Pari Banou Continued

'I do not care how grand the palace was,' the sultan said impatiently when he had heard Nisha's report. 'Or how powerful its owner is. I only care whether Prince Ahmed is safe.'

'I do not believe he is, Your Majesty,' the sorceress replied. 'You cannot trust a genie. And why would Pari Banou hide herself from you unless she was planning something bad? And why would Prince Ahmed hide the fact that he is staying with her unless he was ashamed of it? Or under her spell?'

The sultan sighed. Nisha raised some good points. 'So we still have more questions than answers,' he observed. 'Very well, Ahmed is here right now. It is time to ask him directly. If he cannot or will not talk, then for his own safety I will lock him in his room until I get to the bottom of this.'

'And risk turning him against you further?' Nisha shook her

head. 'Besides, you cannot lock him up forever, Sire, or stop the genie taking revenge if you try.'

'What is to be done, then?'

'If Pari Banou plans to use Ahmed to take your throne, then she will not want you to become stronger. And Prince Ahmed always brings you a gift, which he must get from her. You should ask for one that would improve your chances of success in battle. If the genie lets you have it, then perhaps she can be trusted after all.'

'So I should ask for weapons?'

'Too obvious.'

'Horses?'

'Too easy.' Nisha thought for a minute. 'What about a tent that can fit your entire army inside, but pack away into something small enough to hold in your hand?'

'That sounds impossible,' the sultan said. 'And very, very useful! I will do as you suggest.'

Two days later, Ahmed left. He was eager to see his wife, but his father stopped him at the last minute with his strange request.

'What makes you think I can get

you such a tent?' Ahmed asked.

'Son,' said the sultan, 'I know you do not wish to speak of where you have been, but I understand enough to know that you are staying with someone rich and powerful. Will you not ask that person for me?'

The request made Prince Ahmed very uncomfortable, especially since Pari had said that people always want things from genies. 'Since you know so much already – though I do not know how, I will tell you that "that person" is my wife, father. Is it right for a husband to ask such favours of his wife?

When she has given me her love, should I ask for even more?'

The sultan was surprised to learn of his son's marriage, and even more concerned that he was being controlled by a powerful genie. 'If she loves you so much,' he said, 'she will not deny you.'

When Ahmed returned to the boulder palace, he was not smiling like he usually was.

'What is the matter, my love?' Pari asked him.

'Nothing.'

'Are you unwell?'

'No.'

'Is your father unwell?'

'My father is … my father has asked me to do something I do not want to.' Reluctantly, he explained about the tent.

'And do you think I cannot find such a thing? If that is what is worrying you, then worry no more. Your father shall have his tent. And I shall have a happy husband.'

Ahmed kissed her affectionately. 'I have been happy since the moment we met again. What worries me is that my father should ask for such a thing. It is not like him. And who told him that you have the power to give it to him in the first place?'

'Perhaps it has something to do with the woman you found.'

'What woman?' said Ahmed. 'The one who was injured?'

'I told you, I do not believe she was really injured. She pretended that the fountain water had cured her before it could have. I think she was looking for something – or someone.'

'Who?'

'Me, perhaps. But something tells me there is more to the story. Have you ever seen her in your father's palace?'

Ahmed said that he had not but promised to look out for her the next time he went. When the time for the visit came, he had the tent the sultan wanted.

'But it is too small,' said his father, when they had erected the tent in the palace grounds. Only he and Ahmed were inside it, and it was just big enough to be comfortable.

'It will get bigger or smaller depending on how many are inside,' Ahmed explained, so Prince Ali and Princess Nourinnihar joined them, and afterwards the servants. Then, in his excitement, the sultan commanded his viziers to come inside too. With each new person, the tent expanded. When everyone had piled out again, the sultan was able

to fold it back up into a parcel no bigger than his hand.

'Wonderful!' he cried. 'I will keep this in the treasury.' But outside the treasury, Nisha was waiting to pour more poison in his ear.

'This proves that Ahmed's genie wife is not after my throne,' the sultan said.

'Perhaps,' said Nisha. 'But it also proves that his wife is indeed powerful enough to get him anything he asks for, including your throne. You should test her abilities further ...'

For the second time in as many visits, just as Ahmed was about to return to the boulder palace, his father stopped him. 'Son,' he said, 'will you ask your wife to give me some water from the Fountain of Lions?'

Ahmed frowned. 'How do you know about the Fountain of Lions?'

'You have your secrets,' said the sultan, 'and I have mine.'

'What do you want with the water?' he asked. 'You have the magic apple, which can also heal.'

'The apple is missing.'

'Since when?'

'Since after you left,' the sultan replied, which was true. The apple had disappeared without a trace. 'I am not getting any younger, Ahmed, and I have been feeling my age lately. Surely you care enough about my health to do me this favour?'

This time, when Ahmed returned to Pari he did not wait to tell her of this latest request. 'You were right,' he said. 'That "injured woman" must have been a spy for my father. She told him about you and about the Fountain of Lions. He is completely under her control. I do not think I can go back there.'

'You must,' Pari told him. 'You must save your father from her before she can do any more damage.'

'How?'

'I do not know yet. For now, we will do as he asks – or else she will succeed in turning him against us. Unfortunately, there is no fountain water left. You will have to go get some.'

'How?'

Pari winced. 'That is the difficult part …'

Chapter 9

The Story of Prince Ahmed and Pari Banou Continued

'The Fountain of Lions,' Pari Banou explained, 'is never in the same place. To find where it is now, you must climb the highest hill and unravel this ball of thread from the top.' Then she gave Prince Ahmed two horses: 'One to ride,' she said, 'and never dismount, the other to carry fresh meat. You will understand why when you get there.'

Ahmed set out and did as Pari told him. Trapping one end of the ball of thread under a rock, he rolled the rest from the highest hilltop he could find and followed its path down. It led him to an ancient castle almost swallowed by vines, with walls made thorny by a flowering yellow plant. Only the gate was clear. Beyond it were gardens carpeted with violets and lilies. The sound of trickling water drew Ahmed inside.

He came to a massive fountain with three levels, the top one pouring into the middle and the middle one pouring into the bottom. Nothing poured into the top level and yet it never ran out of water. At each corner of the fountain were four stone lions frozen in a roar.

Ahmed urged his horse forward, pulling at the other. But both animals whinnied and pawed at the ground anxiously, moving every direction but forwards.

'Come on,' Ahmed said impatiently, digging his heels into the horse's side again. It reared up, almost unseating him. He was just considering getting off, despite Pari's warnings not to, when he heard a snarl. Then a definite roar. He looked up. Four flesh-and-blood lions looked back, the four corners of the fountain now empty. Ahmed's horse reared again.

'Whoa there!' he said. The lions crept closer. One licked its lips. *The meat!* Ahmed remembered. Quickly, he grabbed four heavy chunks from the second horse's back and threw them away from the fountain one after the other. The lions ran after the meat and fell upon it with teeth and claws.

'Move!' Ahmed said, urging his frightened horse forward. Without getting off, he leant over the fountain, filling a bottle with water from the second level. He dropped the bottle twice. By the time he was finished, so were the lions. They stalked him to the gate, which had swung closed. Ahmed turned his horse sharply and drew his scimitar. He would fight his way out if he had to.

The lions cocked their heads at him. One yawned. Slowly, Ahmed opened the gate. The lions did nothing but watch, then follow. They followed him all the way to his father's palace, but it was more like they were guarding him than hunting him. They terrified everyone who saw them, then they simply left.

scimitar
A sword with a curved blade that was used in the Middle East.

The sultan was surprised to see Ahmed so soon after his last visit.

'Like you said, father,' Ahmed explained, 'your health is important to me – and to my wife.'

The sultan was very grateful.

He took the bottle from his son and went to show Nisha. 'You were wrong,' he told the sorceress. 'I am in no danger from Ahmed's genie wife. In fact, she is a blessing.'

'How so?' Nisha asked. 'First,

she sends your son home with ten men, then twenty, then thirty – until he had a small army parading through your city. Now she sends him with four lions. What message do you think she is sending, Your Majesty?'

'Message?' the sultan said, kneading his forehead. He really was getting older, and Nisha's words often confused him – just as she intended them to.

'She is *warning* you, Your Majesty. She wants you to fear her power, which she lends to your son.'

'What do you want me to do?' asked the sultan, as if he were not the sultan at all, but a servant. So Nisha smiled and told him.

The next day, before Ahmed could return home, the sultan stopped him. The prince thought he knew what to expect by now, but even he was surprised by the sultan's third request.

'I want you to bring me a man no taller than 140 centimetres, whose beard is nine metres long and who carries an iron bar that weighs 250 kilograms.'

Ahmed could not help himself;

he laughed in his father's face. 'Father, what reason can you have to ask such an impossible thing? To help your army? Improve your health? What?'

But the sultan did not know why Nisha had made such a request, only that she had promised him it was the last one.

When Ahmed returned to the boulder palace, Pari took one look at his face and said: 'What has he asked for now?'

Ahmed explained quickly and complained at length. 'He wants to make a fool of us!' he said. 'He knows we cannot find such a man and he wants to see us fail – or his sorceress does.'

'I do not think so,' Pari disagreed. 'I think we might finally be getting to the bottom of things.'

'Why?' Ahmed demanded.

'Because I know a man of exactly that height, with a beard exactly that length and an iron quarterstaff exactly that heavy … He is my brother.'

'The one who would not come to our wedding?' Ahmed remembered.

quarterstaff
A pole roughly two to three metres long that is used as a weapon.

'The very same.'

'But why would the sorceress want him? How does she even know he exists?'

'I believe we will soon find out. I will call him here now – but I warn you, most people find him quite frightening.'

Pari sent for a box of incense and burnt some on a gold dish. Into the cloud of scented smoke that arose, she whispered the name: 'Schaibar.' Immediately, the smoke thickened into the solid shape of a genie. He was short and muscular,

incense
A substance that makes a nice smell when burnt.

with a beard so long it had to be
wrapped around his body or he
would trip over it. On his head was
a pointed cap. In his hand was an
iron bar. And in his eyes was a look
of fury that chilled Ahmed's blood.

'What is it?' he demanded. 'Who
is this?' He glared up at Ahmed.

'Peace, Schaibar,' Pari soothed, kissing her brother on each cheek. 'This is my husband, Ahmed.'

Schaibar relaxed a little, but he still looked as if he had never smiled in his life. 'And what do you want?'

'My husband's father, the sultan, has made two strange requests since our wedding, and his third involves you. Will you go with Ahmed to his father's palace and settle the matter for me?'

'Very well.'

Chapter 10

The Story of Prince Ahmed and Pari Banou Continued

The next morning, Prince Ahmed and his brother-in-law, Schaibar, walked to the palace. They could not ride because the horses were too scared, and the people they passed found Schaibar more terrifying than the lions. Fury rolled off him like storm clouds, chasing them away. With each step, he banged his quarterstaff down on the ground. By the time they reached the palace, the streets were empty. At the palace gates, even the guards ran. The sultan did not know he had visitors until Ahmed and Schaibar reached his throne room. He was in the middle of talking to his viziers when they all left too. Then there was just him, the prince and the genie.

'Well?' demanded Schaibar. 'You asked for me, and here I am. What do you want?'

But the only reason the sultan had not run was because he was frozen with fear.

'It was not him who asked for you but me,' Nisha called out, hiding in the shadows as usual.

Ahmed watched as Nisha emerged. He recognised her instantly – and so did Schaibar. The genie's face turned pale.

'You!' he gasped.

'*Me,*' said the sorceress. 'I have found you at last after you ran away from me.'

'I told you, I hate weddings!'

A bolt of lightning left the sorceress's hand, striking the floor where Schaibar was standing just before he leapt aside.

'Even your own wedding?' she hissed. 'It was *you* who asked to marry *me*!'

'Well, I changed my mind!'

Another lightning bolt struck. Schaibar responded with his quarterstaff. He hit the floor so hard that a crack split the throne

room, racing towards Nisha
who threw herself out of its path
before it could swallow her.

She seized the
end of Schaibar's
unravelling beard
and dragged him
outside.

'But I love you!' she
screamed.

The genie swung his
staff, nearly taking her
head off. 'I love you too!
I just do not want to get
married!'

More lightning scorched
the air, blackening walls
and setting fire to grass.
'Stop!' shouted Ahmed.

Schaibar swung his quarterstaff
so wildly that he toppled a pillar.
The roof it had been holding up
came crashing down. Ahmed
heard a cry from inside the throne
room. Prince Ali and Princess
Nourinnihar came running to see
what was happening.

'Help father!' Ahmed told them,
as he continued shouting for the
genie and the sorceress to stop.
But they did not.

Schaibar's magic was stronger
but Nisha's fury made up for it.
Plus she had the water from the
Fountain of Lions. Each time she

was injured, the sorceress would drink. By the end of the first half-hour, she was bruised and limping, but by the start of the second, she was as good as new. Unlike Schaibar who remained wounded and bloody.

The fight reached the edge of the palace grounds and threatened to spill out into the streets. With a sudden idea, Ahmed ran to the treasury. He returned with the magic tent and threw it over the couple. Before they could escape, he folded the tent into the palm of his hand. He could still hear them

yelling, but it was a tiny, mousy
sound.

'Stop fighting and talk!' he told
them. 'I will not let you out until
you do.'

Then Ahmed returned to the throne room, where he found Ali and Nour cradling the sultan. He had been injured when the roof fell.

'If only we had the magic apple,' Nour wept. 'We cannot save him without it.'

With another idea, Ahmed ran back into the gardens where he had seen Nisha drop the fountain water during the fight. But when he pressed the bottle to his father's lips, not a single drop was left – and the sultan did not look as if he would live half an hour for it to work anyway.

'Where are you?' he croaked.

'I … I cannot see …' He fumbled weakly for a hand to hold. His eyes were open but unseeing.

'See …' Ali repeated. *'See …'* Then he clapped his hand to his forehead.

'What is it?' asked Ahmed, but his older brother dashed away without answering. He returned with the magic eye glass.

'Show me where the magic apple is,' he demanded as he looked through it.

The apple was found in Nisha's bedroom, along with other random

items from the treasury, and it was swiftly used to save the sultan from death. The family could only assume that the sorceress was not aware of its power when she took it, otherwise she would have used it. But what bothered Ali was that he had almost forgotten about the magic eye glass.

'I thought you were the smart one,' Ahmed teased Ali.

'I thought *I* was the smart one,' came a voice from above them. They looked up to see Prince Hussain floating above their heads on the magic carpet. 'And the handsome one, the funny one, the strong one and–'

'The very, very *late* one,' laughed the sultan. 'Where have you been?'

'Oh, everywhere, father!' The eldest prince joined his family in the throne room, so excited that he seemed not to notice it was in pieces. 'I visited all the royal families like you asked, and I met the most wonderful princess – no offence, Nour – in the whole wide world. We are to be married!'

After the others congratulated him, Hussain finally took in his surroundings. 'So,' he said, 'what did I miss?'

Ahmed wasted no time and took his father to the boulder palace so that he could finally meet Pari Banou. The sultan saw that she

was good and kind and apologised for being convinced otherwise.

'But where is the sorceress?' Pari wondered. 'And where is my brother?'

Ahmed gave her the folded tent. It was not yelling they could hear now but laughter. They left Nisha and Schaibar in there a while longer.

In time, Pari Banou was convinced to leave her palace to visit her husband's family – and even to forgive her brothers-in-law for once insisting that she was imaginary.

Hussain's wedding was grander than Ali's and lasted longer than Ahmed's, but as for who was happiest, even he was willing to call it a draw.